Dear Parents,

As the creator of Go!
the founder of Dream Big Toy Company, I would like
to thank you for giving your child the gifts of
reading and healthy life-skills.

Healthy habits start early. I created
Go! Go! Sports Girls as a fun and educational way
to promote self-appreciation and the benefits
of daily exercise, smart eating and sleeping
habits, self-esteem, and overall healthy life-skills
irls. Author Kara Douglass Thom and
illustrator Pamela Seatter have taken this dream
a step further by creating a series of fun and
educational books to accompany the dolls.
Now your child can Read & Play.

The books have been written for the
child who has begun to read alone, and younger
children will enjoy having the stories read to them.

I believe every child should have the
opportunity to Dream Big and Go For It!

Sincerely,

Jodi Bondi Norgaard

Jodi Bondi Norgaard

For our very own sports girls
Grace, McKenna, Kendall, Jocie Claire,
Kaelie, Maia, and Michaela,
and their brothers Peter, Ben, Blake,
and Alex, who inspire us every day.
— JBN, KDT, PS, SRB

First published in 2014

Series Editor: Susan Rich Brooke

Text © 2014 by Kara Douglass Thom

Illustrations © 2014 by Pamela Seatter

www.gogosportsgirls.com

Library of Congress Control Number: 2013951441

First Edition

8 7 6 5 4 3 2 1

Gymnastics Girl
Maya's Story
Becoming Brave

Written by Kara Douglass Thom

Illustrated by Pamela Seatter

Dream Big Toy Company™

Some girls are born brave. They aren't afraid of the dark. They can watch scary movies. At the amusement park, they get on rides that go high or fast—and keep their eyes open the whole time.

Well, I'm not one of those girls.

I won't go into the basement alone. I don't like thunder. Spiders freak me out.

I'm afraid of Ms. Galvan, the old woman who lives in the creepy house across the street.

When I climb trees with my friend M.C., I stay on the lowest branches—the ones I can jump from and still land on my feet.

Fantastic Gymnastics

Gymnastics started in ancient Greece as a way to improve running, jumping, and wrestling.

Later, the Romans used gymnastics to make their soldiers stronger.

The parallel bars and balance beam were invented in Germany in the early 1800s.

Women's gymnastics first appeared at the Olympics in 1928.

And that's why my parents were totally surprised when I told them I wanted to take gymnastics.

It all started when I watched the Olympics on TV. I was amazed at the flips and jumps and twists and turns the gymnasts could do. And I was amazed that those girls weren't afraid to do them. At least, they didn't look afraid to me. I knew that if I wanted to be a gymnast, I couldn't be afraid either. I would need to become brave.

I asked my mom and dad if I could take gymnastics lessons. I asked again, and again. They thought I only liked the *idea* of being a gymnast. It took forever to convince them that I really wanted to try gymnastics, even if it meant doing things that scared me.

Get in Gear

To do gymnastics, you'll need: a leotard, hand grips or chalk to keep from slipping on the bars, and a hair band to pull back your hair.

I signed up for the Super Beginner class, instead of the Beginner class, because I already knew how to do a forward roll and a cartwheel. And I could walk across the balance beam without falling. Well, the balance beam was only six inches off the floor, so I didn't have far to fall. Nothing was too scary in that class. I learned how to do a back bend and a backward roll.

For the next session, I moved to the Intermediate level. With my coach spotting me, I tried things that were a little bit scarier, like a forward roll from a handstand, and a round off.

Once I got into the Advanced level, though, I wondered how I would ever make the Olympic team. The skills—walkover, handspring, squat on—were so much harder, and scarier.

A squat on is a skill on the uneven bars. You have to stand up from a squat on the low bar, and then jump up to the high bar. My hands never wanted to let go of the low bar, and I would lose my balance and fall backward. Coach said that I should keep my hands and feet on the bar and swing around until I get back to the top. That's called a sole circle.

If only I could get my hips higher, I could find my balance on the low bar before leaping. Coach said I would have to be quick. And I would have to be fearless.

It seemed impossible. And so did doing a handspring without the big round wedge that helped me flip over without falling.

Vault

Balance beam

The Big Events

Uneven bars

Floor exercise

11

One day, on the way home from gymnastics practice, I saw something strange on our street.

"Mom! Look at all the cars in front of Ms. Galvan's house," I exclaimed.

As long as I can remember, I had never seen a visitor at Ms. Galvan's home. I'd barely even seen Ms. Galvan behind that tall fence that surrounds her house. I'd been afraid of her ever since Kevin and James down the street told me she was a mean old witch. None of the kids would trick-or-treat there. They told me that if I walked on the sidewalk in front of her house, she would cast a spell on me. So of course I never walked in front of her house.

"Ms. Galvan just got home from the hospital," my mom said as we pulled into the driveway. "I'm taking a spinach lasagna over to her house now. Do you want to come?"

I didn't say no to my mom, but I didn't say yes, either. I just darted up the stairs to my room and hoped she wouldn't ask me again. Then I watched Mom carry the casserole dish across the street, go through the open gate, and stand in front of Ms. Galvan's door.

Please don't put a curse on my mom, I thought, as my heart pounded through my leotard. I didn't look away from the window until I saw Mom hand over the dish and head back home.

That night, I had trouble falling asleep. When I finally did, I dreamed about Ms. Galvan. We were both standing on the low bar. She winked at me, and we jumped up to the high bar together. I don't know if we made it, because a huge clap of thunder woke me up before I finished the dream.

BOOM!

The storm made me too scared to fall back asleep. And I couldn't stop thinking about Ms. Galvan. Since it didn't seem like my mom was suffering from a curse, I decided to make Ms. Galvan a card. I wrote "Get Well Soon" on it with my best markers, and I decorated it with stickers.

17

As I walked slowly up Mrs. Galvan's walk the next day, I saw Kevin and James peeking through the fence. I felt brave—but not brave enough to ring the doorbell. I opened the mailbox, and just as I dropped the card in... Ms. Galvan opened the door!

"Yes, child?"

"I... I... I..." I couldn't get another word out of my mouth.

"Sorry to startle you, dear," Ms. Galvan said. The door was open only as wide as her face.

After I caught my breath, I realized I wasn't afraid. Through the narrow opening in the door, the most beautiful eyes stared back at me. They were so dark blue they were almost purple. And they were kind.

"You must be Maya, from across the street,"
Mrs. Galvan said. "Are you here to pick up the
casserole dish?"

"No, ma'am. I'm here to give you this."
I reached into the mailbox and handed her the
card. She looked at it for a long time. Then she
opened the door wider.

"Why don't you come in, dear?"

I took a deep breath and followed her inside.
"Thank you for the beautiful card, Maya,"
Ms. Galvan said as she poured a cup of chocolate
milk for me and some coffee for herself. "My
neighbors have been so helpful through my
illness. I didn't know how kind you all were.
I guess I haven't gotten to know many people."

"But you've lived here a long time," I found myself saying.

"I prefer to be indoors, in my home," Ms. Galvan said. "I don't like going outside much."

"But why?" I asked.

"I suppose..." Ms. Galvan held her coffee mug tighter and glanced out the window. "I suppose I'm just afraid."

"Afraid of what?"

Ms. Galvan turned her kind purple eyes toward me. I felt ashamed for believing she was a witch.

"I don't know!" she said. Then she laughed, which made me laugh, too. "Isn't that silly?"

I nodded my head, and we laughed together some more.

The next week, after
I helped my mom make a
batch of maple nut granola,
I surprised her by offering
to take some to Ms. Galvan.
When I crossed the
street, *I* got a surprise:
Ms. Galvan was sitting
on her front porch!

"You're outside!" I said.

"Yes," Mrs. Galvan said. "I've been practicing. I figure the more I get outside, the easier it will get."

"That's how I feel about gymnastics," I said. "I'm afraid to do a front handspring by myself. But I practice every week anyway." 23

I kept practicing my handsprings. And I noticed Mrs. Galvan outside more. Mom and I had brought her a flowerpot to put on her porch. She went out often to admire the snapdragons.

"The more I leave my house, the more I discover I like it out here," Ms. Galvan said one afternoon as we sat together on her swing. "Listen to the birds chirping. Look at that beautiful spiderweb on the ceiling."

My heart thumped. *Spider?!?*

"I suppose when something becomes more familiar," Ms. Galvan continued, "well, then, what's there to be frightened of?"

It was true: the longer I forced myself to look at the spider, the less scary it seemed. I wondered if the Olympic gymnasts were scared of the balance beam or uneven bars when they first tried them.

"How's that front handspring?" Ms. Galvan asked, after the spider crawled away. "Are you still afraid to try it?"

"No," I said, "as long as I flip over the foam roll that supports my back."

"So it's a little like me going outside, but still staying behind these gates, isn't it?" Ms. Galvan asked.

PROPERTY
OF
THE GYM

The Scoop on Scores

Nadia Comaneci is a Romanian gymnast famous for scoring the first "perfect 10" at the 1976 Olympics. In 2005, gymnastics scoring changed. Now gymnasts get an "A score" for difficulty (how hard each skill is that they do) and a "B score" for execution (how well they perform their routines). With the new system, there is no perfect score. As gymnasts perform harder routines, the top scores will rise.

At the next gymnastics lesson, I ran toward the foam roll and did my handspring. My teacher looked at me, and I could tell she was thinking the same thing I was thinking: I was ready to try a handspring on my own.

I ran down the mat, raised my arms, brought them down, and pushed my body skyward. My legs stretched toward the ceiling and flipped around behind me. I imagined that the roll was underneath me, holding me up.

When my feet touched the mat, I hopped and came back down with my arms high above my head, the way Olympic gymnasts do.

I smiled a big smile when I realized I had done it—I had landed on my feet!

The morning of the big meet, I looked frantically for my favorite leotard. It's bright orange with swirls of blue, pink, purple, and green. I was sure it would bring me good luck. I *had* to wear it.

"Mom!" I called, with my head still under the bed. "I can't find it anywhere!"

"It's in the dryer in the basement," she shouted back. "I'll go get it—" But I had already raced past her and down the stairs.

When I came back up, clutching my leotard, Mom was standing at the top of the stairs. Her jaw was dropped and her eyes were wide.

"What?" I asked casually, as if I'd always gone into the basement by myself.

29

At the end of the gymnastics meet, I stood proudly on the podium holding my first ribbon. I smiled out at the audience. My parents were there, cheering for me. My friend M.C. was there, too.

And so was Ms. Galvan. She was brave for coming to my meet. I was brave for doing the handspring that helped me earn my ribbon. I caught her kind eyes, and she winked at me— just like in my dream, when we were standing on the low bar, and we jumped up to the high bar together.

In real life, I still need to practice my squat on. But now, I know how the dream is going to end: we'll be brave.

Meet and Compete

At a meet, gymnasts do different routines for each event. Competitions for each event take place at the same time, so it's a little like watching a "four-ring" circus. For each event, the gymnast with the highest score gets an individual award. The "All-Around" title goes to the gymnast with the highest total score for all events. Gymnasts' total scores are combined for the team competition. The team with the most points wins.

Here's What Maya Learned:

- You can't change some things about yourself, like the color of your eyes or the size of your feet. But you can change other things, like being more helpful, learning new skills, or becoming brave.

- The more familiar you become with something that scares you, the less scary it will seem.

- The word IMPOSSIBLE also spells I'M POSSIBLE. Anything's possible if you take time to learn and practice.

Gymnastics Girl Maya's Healthy Tips:

- Spot on. When you learn new gymnastics skills, always have a coach help you.

- Warm up. Before practice, Maya runs around the gym, bends side to side, reaches to the sky, touches her toes, and does sit ups.

- Fuel in. Natural snacks like berries or sunflower seeds give you more energy than sugary snacks.

- Drink up. To replace the water you lose when you sweat, make sure you drink water, not sodas or sugary drinks.

- Lights out. Get lots of sleep every night, especially before a gymnastics meet.

Dream Big and Go For It!

Made in the USA
Middletown, DE
19 December 2024

67888424R00020